*To Liz, Sam, Steve, Amos, Schisseli und Bowli, and
horse lovers everywhere.*
—R. A.

For my sister Ann who always did ride better than I did.
—P. P.

Thanks to all my models, with a special thanks to Nate Hathaway,

who posed as the young boy throughout the story.

—P. P.

Atheneum Books for Young Readers
An imprint of Simon & Schuster Children's Publishing Division
1230 Avenue of the Americas
New York, New York 10020

Text copyright © 2001 by Richard Ammon
Illustrations copyright © 2001 by Pamela Patrick

The text of this book is set in Weiss.
The illustrations are rendered in pastels.
Printed in Hong Kong

2 4 6 8 10 9 7 5 3 1

Library of Congress Cataloging-in-Publication Data
Ammon, Richard.
Amish horses / by Richard Ammon ; illustrated by Pamela Patrick.—1st ed.
p. cm.
Summary: An Amish boy cares for the horses that work on his family's farm.
ISBN 0-689-82623-0
[1. Amish—Fiction. 2. Horses—Fiction. 3. Farm life—Pennsylvania—Fiction. 4. Pennsylvania—Fiction.] I. Patrick, Pamela,
ill. II. Title.
PZ7.A5165 Ap 2001
[Fic]—dc21 99-089452

AMISH HORSES

by RICHARD AMMON
illustrated by PAMELA PATRICK

ATHENEUM BOOKS FOR YOUNG READERS
NEW YORK   LONDON   TORONTO   SYDNEY   SINGAPORE

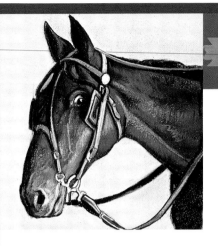

Ever since I was old enough to help with the chores, I've cared for our horses. Datt says that I have a special way with them. Because we Amish do not drive cars, trucks, or tractors, our horses are very important to us.

They whinny as I enter the stable. "*Gut Marriye* (Good Morning), Ben. *Gut Marriye,* Jerry," I say as I pour scoopfuls of oats in their trough. Ben and Jerry are Belgians, draft horses that work the field, taking the place of tractors. We stable them together because they work together. Our other draft horses are another pair of Belgians, Rowdy and Buster, and two Percherons, Judy and Rock.

Roy, a Saddlebred who pulls our *Doch Waggle* (buggy), nickers. He's telling me that he's hungry, too. "I haven't forgotten you," I tell Roy as I break open a bale of hay and throw some in his trough.

After school, I clean out their stalls, shoveling manure into the wheelbarrow to dump near Memm's garden. Manure makes good fertilizer.

Later in the evening, I currycomb each horse. "Ei, yi, yi, Ben! How did you get so matted?" I ask as I comb dirt from his blond mane and tail and brush his coat until it's silky.

One evening in early spring, I open the stall and lead Ben to the water trough, an old bathtub filled with running water. Two blue-gills swim out of the way of the slurping horse. Refreshed, Ben leans his one-ton body against me. That's horse talk meaning we're friends. I stretch my arm along his withers. "Yes, Ben, we're buddies."

Ben drops his head to let me slip on his bridle.

In the cool evening I lead Ben to Memm's garden. After I fasten the harness to the plow, my little sister, Lizzie, comes running over. I lift her onto the horse's back.

"Giddyap," she says. As Ben pulls, I guide the plow up one row and down the next.

Then we hitch Ben to the disk and harrow to break up the deep furrows, making the garden soil as fine and smooth as sand. Tomorrow, Memm can begin planting. Datt can't wait for spring onions and radishes.

In late May, safely past a chance of frost, it's time to plant tomatoes, a whole field of tomatoes! Judy, our dapple gray Percheron, neighs as I open the gate to her stall. "How are you, big girl?" I ask, patting her along her thick neck.

I hitch Judy and her partner, Rock, a black Percheron, to the planter. My older sisters, Rachel and Fannie, sit in front of the planter with their legs stretched out straight, holding a flat of tomato plants.

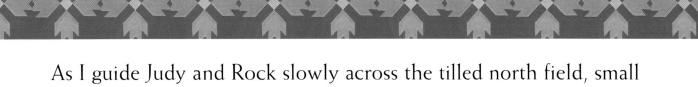

As I guide Judy and Rock slowly across the tilled north field, small wheels at the front of the planter poke holes and squirt water into the ground. Fannie and Rachel push young tomato stalks into the moist pockets of earth.

Barefoot, Lizzie walks behind, scooping soil around any plants that may have fallen over. Later, she sits on the back of the planter, dragging her feet in the fine earth.

Making hay begins with mowing the alfalfa. I harness Ben and Jerry to a small cart hooked to the mower and crimper. Giving the lines a snap, I call, "Giddyap," and the pair tramps off to the south field.

As I mow, the crimper trails behind, wringing moisture from the grass so it dries more quickly. There's not much to do riding in the cart. Ben and Jerry obediently follow the rows and even know to turn at the end of the field. In the middle of the afternoon, when the sun is high, I feel drowsy.

I unhitch Ben and Jerry and lead them to the creek at the bottom of the south field. There I splash my face with water while they stand under the shade of the willow, taking a long, cool drink.

The next morning after the dew is off the hay, I hitch Rowdy and Buster to the rake that whirls and churns the hay into long, neat rows.

We need all six draft horses to pull the hay baler and wagon. I hitch Judy to the left of the tongue, making her the lead horse. All the other horses will follow her.

After lunch, Rachel snaps the lines, and Judy steps off, leading the team to the south field. I ride the hay wagon, which sways, bounces, pitches, and lurches over the bumpy field.

Standing on the wagon, I grab bales shooting from the baler and stack them like toy blocks. My eyes water from the dust. The scratchy hay turns my arms red and raw, and the baling twine cuts into my hands. I grunt as I lift a bale above my head, shoving it high atop the load.

Just about the time the wagon is full, I see Uncle Elam coming to help. His pair of mules is pulling an empty hay wagon. Elam prefers mules because they are strong, hard workers that don't eat very much, and can stand the heat better than most horses. But he admits that sometimes they can be stubborn.

Elam switches his empty wagon for a full one and drives it to the barn, where he helps Datt stack the bales in the loft.

Rachel and I continue baling throughout the long day. The setting sun shimmers glorious reds and brilliant oranges as we drive the team to the barn, where Rachel and I feed and water each twosome in their stalls.

That evening at the picnic table under the maple tree, Memm dishes out ice cream. The talk is about how much hay we made, and what we must do tomorrow. "That reminds me," Datt says. "In the morning I must take Roy to Dan Zook's." He's the farrier who will fit Roy with new shoes. Some day I'd like to be a farrier.

"May I go along?" I ask hopefully.

"As long as you do all your chores first."

The next morning after feeding the horses, I hitch Roy to the *Schpring Wagge* (spring wagon). Datt lets me drive. Roy trots down the road, his ears pointed forward. But near the junkyard, he slows, lays his ears back, and turns his head.

"Roy sure doesn't like those junk cars at the garage," I remind Datt. "Giddyap," I call, holding the lines loosely, and Roy quickens his pace, past the junkers, through the covered bridge, around the bend to Dan Zook's place.

"How's our big fellow today?" Dan asks, patting Roy's neck. Talking gently, he lifts Roy's front foot. First, he removes the old horseshoe and trims the hoof, which is like trimming fingernails and doesn't hurt Roy one bit. Next, Dan measures Roy's hoof and selects the right-sized shoe from hundreds hanging from the rafters. After heating the shoe, he hammers it into shape. Then Dan plunges the red-hot shoe into a water barrel before nailing it onto Roy's hoof.

Almost too soon, Roy is wearing four new shoes. I wish we could spend the morning at Dan's but there's more hay to bale.

We wave to Dan as Roy struts out the lane, almost as if he's showing off his new shoes.

One Sunday when we don't have church, Datt announces, "Let's visit Anna and Samuel." My sisters fly around, putting on stockings and shoes and slipping into the dresses and matching capes they pressed last evening.

Snatching my straw hat from the hooks, I run to hitch Roy to our gray buggy. Then I climb in the back with my sisters.

Datt cracks the lines. Roy, holding his head up and his ears forward, high-steps down the road through the valley brimming with fields of golden wheat and knee-high corn. Then it's over the mountain. Roy slows to a walk as we creep up the steep road. Near a spring along the road, Datt pulls off to the side to let Roy rest. While everyone drinks from the spring, I fill the bucket I brought along. With a heave, I toss the water onto Roy's back to cool him.

After a while, we roll down the mountain and across the next valley to my sister's home.

Dust spirals from buggy wheels. It's Melvin driving a pair of Standardbreds. He's come to see Rachel. *Grossdawdi* (Grandfather) must have told him that we are at Anna's.

Many Standardbreds were raised for horse racing, so I say to Melvin, *"Die Gaul kanne geh verhafdich* (Your horses can really go)."

"I like when my Standardbreds stick out their necks and run! None of this prancing like your Saddlebred," he says with a good-natured smile.

"How'd they do coming over the mountain?" Datt asks.

"No problem," Melvin says. "They slowed up a bit, but they didn't need to stop."

Smiling, Rachel comes from the house and climbs into the open buggy. "Giddyap," Melvin calls, and off they go to a singing with their friends.

"Maybe we need to get Roy some help," Datt says to me.

I smile at the thought of getting a new horse. I hope Datt takes me along to the auction.

On the day of the horse auction, Uncle Amos drives his Morgan down our lane. "Whoa, Raven," Amos says, pulling up near the barn.

The Morgan is so small, I ask, "Can she pull as much as our Roy?"

Amos grins. "Morgans have large chests and powerful legs. Raven can pull *more* than your Roy."

"She's a beauty," I say, admiring her glistening black coat, long mane, and tail.

With the screen door slamming behind him, Datt hurries to Amos's wagon. *"Graddle nei* (Crawl in)," he says to me.

In an instant, I leap in, excited to be going along.

We tie Raven under a long shed with other Amish and Mennonite buggies. Datt and Amos head straight for the sales barn.

Moving slowly from stall to stall, Datt carefully looks over each horse. He crosses several horses from his list. One has glassy eyes. "They just don't pay attention," he says. Another's feet point out. "He'll be too hard to drive."

At the next stall Datt looks directly into the horse's eyes. Walking away he says, "His eyes tell me he's too headstrong." I wasn't sure how Datt could tell, but Datt does know his horses.

"What about this one?" I ask at the stall of a tall Standardbred.

"He's a beauty. I know Melvin likes Standardbreds and they make good drivers, but I think you want one that can be a pet, too, like Roy."

I smile, knowing Datt understands.

When Datt and Amos run into their old friend Abner, they talk like they haven't seen each other for years. I practically have to drag Datt to the arena where the sale is about to begin.

As handlers lead the horses one by one down the run, the auctioneer announces the name, age, and condition of each. "This three-gaiter cribs a little," he says.

Datt crosses this horse from his list. He says, "We don't want one that chews on his stall."

Time moves slowly. No horse seems right. I wonder whether we will find a horse today.

Datt recognizes a dealer. "Maybe Chris brought some horses from Kentucky."

"Two for one," the auctioneer announces. My heart races as Chris leads a beautiful, chestnut mare with a *Hutscheli* (foal) glued to her side.

With a wave of his list, Datt enters the bidding. But just as quickly, the bids soar higher than the rafters, and my heart sinks.

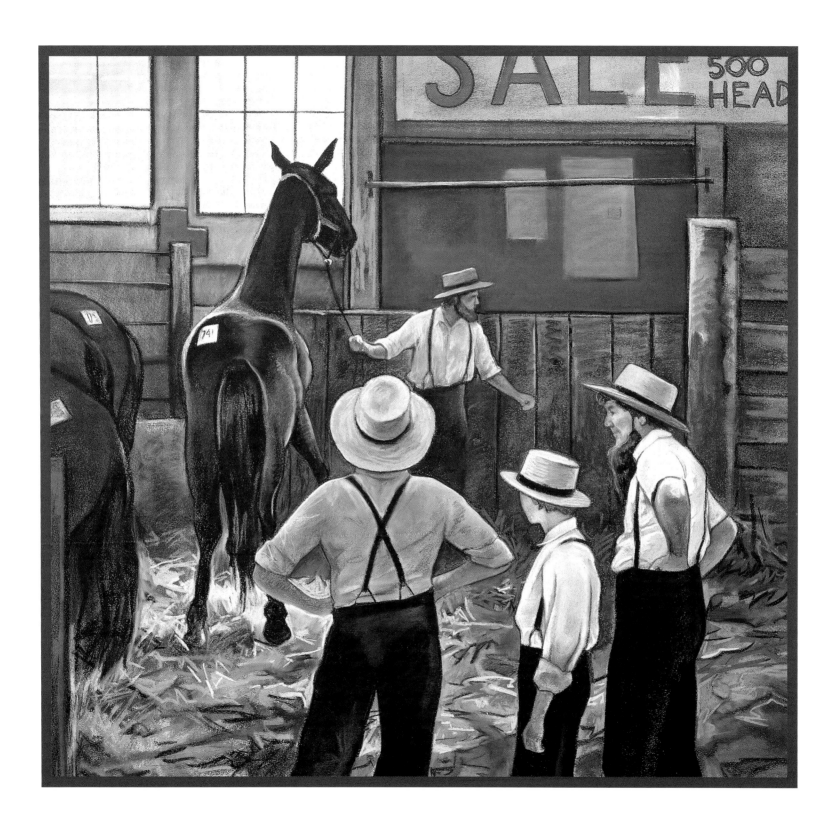

My disappointment evaporates when a handsome black gelding enters the ring. The auctioneer calls out, "This horse is selling okay." That means that the vet found no problems.

The auctioneer begins his bouncy, fast-talking singsong.

My eyes are glued on Datt. He nods. The bid-taker yells, "Yeaaah!"

Others bid, too. "I've got fourteen who'll give fifteen bumpity-bumpity-bumpity fifteen-fifteen-fifteen who'll give me fifteen?"

Datt lifts his little finger. "Yeaaah!" calls the bid-taker.

"Fifteen who'll give me sixteen-sixteen-sixteen bumpity-bumpity-bumpity sixteen-sixteen-sixteen. . . . "

Soon it's down to two bidders. Back and forth the bidding goes between Datt and a man in a plaid shirt.

I worry that the bidding will go too high for Datt.

Datt winks.

"Yeaaah!" cries the bid-taker.

The auctioneer looks at the man in the plaid shirt. He shakes his head sideways.

BAM! The auctioneer raps his gavel. "Sold!" he says, pointing to Datt.

While Datt goes to the office to pay, I hurry to the horse's stall, put on his halter, and tie him to the back of Amos's buggy. As our new horse trots behind, I talk to him gently all the way home.

That evening at dinner Datt asks, "What should we name our new horse?"

I had thought of Black Beauty. My little sister, Lizzie, wanting to join the conversation and thinking of Roy, her favorite, blurts out, "*Vell, net Roy* (Well, not Roy)!"

"*Ferwas net Netroy* (Why not Netroy)?" I ask.

My older brother, Jake, laughs. Rachel and Fannie giggle.

But Datt says, "Netroy is different than Star or Sonny. No one else in the valley has a horse named Netroy."

"Datt, no one else in the *world* has a horse named Netroy," Jake says, shaking his head.

"Then Netroy it is," Datt says.

That evening after chores, I hear Netroy squeal. Datt says, "I put the other horses out to pasture, and he wants to be there, too. But he doesn't know where the fence is yet, and I'm afraid he might break through."

I go to Netroy's stall. When he sees me, he squeals some more, turns his rump, and kicks wildly. Slowly, I open the gate and quickly slip a halter over his head. Almost immediately he settles down. I walk him around our place. He pauses every so often, unsure where he is. I talk gently to him, coaxing him on. I lead him around the pasture fence so he learns his boundaries.

As we return through the gate, I step back to admire his looks. Then I grab his mane and fling myself onto his bare back. I nudge him past the barn and down the dirt lane. Reaching the crest of the hill, I squeeze my thighs against Netroy's flanks to urge him into a trot.

Datt appears from the barn and notices a plume of dust rising from behind the crown of the hay field. "Lydia," he calls to Memm, weeding the garden, *"Guck emol do* (Look at that)*!"*

My hat sails behind as Netroy gallops along the ridge of the hill. I have a new friend.

Author's Note

The idea for this story came to me when I drove three Old Order Amish friends to the Saddlebred horse sale in Lexington, Kentucky.

With my Amish neighbors, I have experienced or observed everything that happened in this book. For example, in order to be accurate in the hay-making scenes, I actually worked in the fields with Amish. Again, as in earlier books, my Amish friends have read the story and examined the art for accuracy.

Glossary

BELGIAN: A kind of draft, or workhorse, that is very tall, reaching about seventeen hands and weighing almost a ton. Very strong, yet good-natured. Coloring is light chestnut with a blond tail and mane.

COLT: A young male horse.

CRIBBING: A horse's habit of chewing wood or anything in its stall. The horse may also inhale large amounts of air. Some people who know horses say that cribbing is a result of boredom.

FILLY: A female horse less than four years old.

GAIT: The way a horse moves: walk, trot, canter, and gallop. Saddlebreds are also taught to rack, in which they hold their heads up and lift their legs.

GELDING: A male horse that is not able to produce offspring.

HANDS: A unit of measurement used to determine a horse's height. The measurement is from the ground to the highest point of the horse's withers. A hand equals four inches.

MARE: A female horse more than four years old.

MORGAN: So named because all Morgans are descended from a colt owned by Justin Morgan in 1793. Morgans are small, about fourteen to fifteen hands high, compact, with powerful shoulders, and thick necks. They also have thick manes and tails. Ideal family horses, they are surprisingly strong and remarkably fast.

MULE: The offspring of a male donkey and a female horse. They have the speed and strength of their mothers and the patience and sure-footedness of their fathers. Mules are hard workers. It is said that George Washington popularized the mule in America.

PERCHERON: Originating from Normandy, a part of France, this very large draft, or workhorse, ranges from fifteen to eighteen hands high. They are intelligent, easy to handle, and willing to work. Most Percherons are gray, dapple gray, or black.

SADDLEBRED: A spirited, but very kind, gentle, and even affectionate horse. Often bred for the showring.

STALLION: An ungelded male horse more than four years old.

STANDARDBRED: The fastest pacing and trotting horse. These horses are often raced, pulling an ultralight two-wheeled sulky cart with a driver. Standardbreds are easy to handle, willing, and enthusiastic.

WITHERS: The part of the horse at the base of the neck, where the neck joins the body, above the shoulders.